THE
TRAIN MOUSE

First published in English in 2020 by
Andersen Press Limited
20 Vauxhall Bridge Road
London SW1V 2SA
www.andersenpress.co.uk

2 4 6 8 10 9 7 5 3 1

Originally published in German with illustrations by Axel Scheffler as Die Zugmaus
in 2018 by dtv Verlagsgesellschaft mbH & Co. KG, Munich

The translation of this work was supported by a grant from the Goethe-Institut

British Library Cataloguing in Publication Data available.

Hardback ISBN: 978 1 78344 958 3
Paperback ISBN: 978 1 83913 010 6

Printed and bound in China by 1010

THE
TRAIN MOUSE

Uwe Timm

Illustrated by Axel Scheffler
Translated by Rachel Ward

Ⓐ

ANDERSEN PRESS

CHAPTER ONE

'Where did you go for all that time?'

'Did you really go to Paris?'

'Where did you hide on the train?'

I get asked the same questions every day, and then I have to tell everyone about my adventures all over again. I'm even receiving letters now, asking me the easiest way to travel to Paris.

So, to save having to keep explaining it all, I've decided to write my story down.

I'm an ordinary house mouse and my name's Stefan. But everyone calls me Nibbles. How did I end up with such a funny nickname? Well, when I was very young,

I had a habit of gnawing tree trunks, just like a beaver. My parents were puzzled. Sometimes my father wondered if I was even a proper mouse at all. But then, as I got older, all the gnawing suddenly stopped. I must have realised that my little mouse-teeth could never fell a tree.

I was born in the city of Munich in Germany, on Paradise Street. In case you were thinking I made that name up, you can have a look at a map of Munich and then you'll see: *Paradise Street*. It's a real street. But, sadly, the house I was born in is no longer there.

It was such a beautiful old house, surrounded by new, and very tall, buildings. Behind our house there was a little courtyard and, in the yard, there were two elderberry bushes.

We, the mouse family, lived in the cellar of the house: my mother, my father, my grandfather and my brothers and sister. My brothers are called Big Tooth, Short Tail and White Paw, and my little sister is Lilyfey.

Above us lived an old man whose name was Mr Ehlers, and he had a cat named Carlo. Sometimes you could hear a dreadful screeching and barking in the yard.

 2

That meant that Isengrim had come down and was chasing Carlo.

Isengrim was a poodle and he lived in the attic with an artist called Mr Kringel. Mr Kringel painted pictures and liked to eat cheese and white bread. That made him very popular with us mice. Isengrim used to be in a circus and he'd seen a lot of the world. He could walk on two legs and sometimes, if we mice-children asked him, he'd do a somersault for us. He was very friendly to us mice and got on well with all kinds of creatures – except cats. He hated cats. And that wasn't just because he was a dog. There was another reason for that.

You see, Isengrim had spent two years performing in the circus with a cat. The cat lay in a pram wearing a baby's bonnet and Isengrim, who was wearing a little white dress, had to push her around the ring. Although the cat would always hiss nasty remarks at him, no fur was allowed to fly: he just had to keep on pushing her around in a circle in front of the whole audience.

Then, one evening, he could contain himself no longer. She'd whispered: 'My goodness, Isengrim, you look so silly in that short dress with your crooked legs.'

3

So he'd let go of the pram and sprung at her. The cat leaped out of the pram and ran into the rows of seats. Isengrim chased her through the circus tent. The people jumped up, laughing and screaming.

Isengrim wasn't allowed to perform any more after that, and the ringmaster sold him to Mr Kringel.

That was why Carlo the tomcat suffered – for the malice of the circus cat. Isengrim was normally calm and friendly, but his eyes glittered dangerously whenever he spotted Carlo: 'A cat is a cat – they're all the same,' he'd say furiously.

We agreed with him.

But Carlo was really old by then and, to tell the truth, he was very friendly. My grandad sometimes said, 'Leave old Carlo alone, he's worn his claws right out these days.'

Grandad and Carlo had grown up together in the house on Paradise Street.

Grandad also used to say, 'Once upon a time, in the old days, Carlo was a very dangerous mouser. He used to sit outside a mousehole for hours, quiet as a mouse himself. And then, when you thought he couldn't

5

possibly still be there and you crept out, his claws would strike, as fast as lightning. That's how I lost all my brothers and sisters.'

Then Grandad would sit silently for a moment before continuing, 'Carlo almost got me once. I was just about able to dive into a mousehole, but I didn't pull my tail in in time – *tcha* – and he bit it off.'

And every time he told us about the dangers of cats, he'd hold up his stumpy tail as a warning: 'Cats are dangerous.'

But, like I said, Carlo had grown old by then. And old Mr Ehlers bought him plenty of meat from the butcher. So the cat spent most of his time sitting sated and sleepy on the windowsill, warming his old paws in the sun.

But sometimes – only rarely – the passion for hunting would seize him. Then he'd suddenly run after one of us mice, but only slowly, as if he were dreaming. All the same, we mouse-children were only allowed into the yard if Grandad or Isengrim was there.

Then Grandad would sit in the sun too, beside Carlo but not too close, and the two elderly animals would chat, talking about how things used to be.

CHAPTER TWO

The days passed, one much like another. Mum and Dad grated cheese in Mr Kringel's dining room. Grandad dozed beside Carlo in the sun. And we sat around and were sometimes bored. Then we'd go to Isengrim and ask him to tell us about the wide world. About Paris, where there were so many kinds of cheese. And about Switzerland, which was heaven for mice.

Isengrim said, 'You know the cheese with the big holes, don't you? That's Swiss cheese. And do you know how the holes get into the cheese?'

Isengrim paused for a moment, every time. And,

although we'd heard the story plenty of times before, we'd always answer: 'No.'

'The holes are skilfully gnawed out by Swiss mice,' Isengrim would say solemnly. 'So skilfully that there's not the smallest mousy toothmark to be seen.'

And all our little mouse-mouths would water.

'In Switzerland,' Isengrim continued, 'mice are highly-esteemed artisans called cheese-nibblers, but they have to pass an exam first.'

Mice must live a glorious life in Switzerland, we thought, but life was so monotonous here in the yard with the tired, old cat. Then we'd sprawl around wondering who we could play a trick on.

'Come on,' I said to my brother White Paw one day, 'let's play bullfighting with Carlo the Cat.'

'Let's not,' said White Paw. 'For an old tom he can still be pretty speedy sometimes.'

Carlo lay dozing in the sun. I crept quietly up to him. Then I darted forward and pulled one of his whiskers. '*Olé!*' I cried.

The cat leaped up, hissed and arched his back fearsomely. He must have thought Isengrim had been

taunting him. Then he saw me and spat, 'Was that you, titch?'

'Yes, old Tom,' I laughed. 'You can't catch me!'

'Even the pipsqueaks are cheeking me now,' he snarled as he pounced.

My goodness, his teeth seemed huge all of a sudden!

I zig-zagged wildly away. The cat ran after me.

I climbed over a crate. The cat cleared it in one bound. He could still jump so far! I ran across the yard

to the shed. I could already hear the cat wheezing right by my left ear as I slipped through a little crack in the shed. The boards shook under the impact of Carlo's head as he crashed into them.

'*Olé!*' I shouted.

But soon Carlo's taloned paw came through the crack. I was slightly alarmed at how far he could stretch it. I had to jump away from the paw as it swung to and fro. But he couldn't grab me that way, so he sat down in front of the crack. After a while, he disappeared.

My brother yelled something, but I couldn't hear what he was saying. I thought to myself, Wait a moment longer and then you can creep out. I whistled a little song to help drive away the fear. In the end I plucked up the courage to peer out of the crack. And I saw the cat's shadow on the ground. He'd climbed onto a branch hanging down from the elderberry bush and was hiding up there.

At long last, Grandad arrived and I heard him say, 'Carlo, be sensible and come down from that branch. If you jump from there, you'll probably break a paw. At our age we can't jump like we used to.'

 10

'We'll see about that,' answered Carlo angrily.

'Don't let a child annoy you. It was just a silly practical joke,' said Grandad.

'It's the principle of the thing,' spat Carlo. 'I won't be made a fool of by any mouse, let alone a little whippersnapper like Nibbles.'

And Carlo kept on sitting there on that branch.

So that was why I was still cowering in the shed when evening came and it got cold. I thought about how nice it would be to be sitting in the cellar with my brothers and sister, eating some of the cheese that Mum and Dad had brought from Mr Kringel's attic.

Then old Mr Ehlers came and called: 'Carlo!'

He spotted him in the elderberry bush and called, 'Silly old chap, what are you doing up there? Climbed up and can't get down again, eh?'

Old Mr Ehlers lifted the cat from the branch. I saw the old tom stalk stiffly into the kitchen where his food bowl was.

Carlo had barely vanished into the house when I heard Dad's voice by the crack. 'Come out,' he called.

He took me down to the cellar. 'What a silly thing

to do. Leave old Carlo alone and then he'll leave us be and we can all live in peace.'

I had to go straight to bed after supper as a punishment. I lay in my warm nest and felt glad that I'd escaped from the draughty old shed in one piece.

Grandad dropped in on me and told me about the old days when hardly anyone had a fridge. People still had larders in those days, and the cheese lay in the larders wrapped up in damp cloths. Those were the days!

I soon drifted off to sleep.

CHAPTER THREE

Apart from little adventures like that, we all lived peacefully without a thought for tomorrow. And so week after week passed, and month after month. Until one day there was a great uproar in the house.

Mr Kringel the artist was painting placards instead of pictures. They said: *THIS HOUSE STAYS* and *SAVE THIS CONSTRUCTION FROM SENSELESS DESTRUCTION!*

Mr Kringel hung the placards out of the windows. In the evenings, he had meetings with old Mr Ehlers. They both went quite red in the face, what with all the wine and the excitement.

13

Old Mr Ehlers kept saying, 'We have to resist!'

'They can't just treat us however they like,' said Mr Kringel.

But then, three weeks later, the artist moved out. When Isengrim came to say goodbye, he told us that the artist had bought an old house in the countryside. He planned to paint in peace out there. That was a serious blow to us because we had lost our breadwinner in that fan of red wine and French cheese.

And then, one day, old Mr Ehlers began packing up his things too.

Carlo the cat came to take his leave of Grandad.

He said, 'We're moving to what they call a new-build. On the ninth floor!'

'Oh, how nice,' I exclaimed, 'you'll have a great view of the world.'

But Carlo muttered sadly, 'I won't be able to jump down into the yard from up there. And I won't be able to lie on the windowsill either.'

That afternoon, the removal van came. The cupboards, chairs and beds were carried out. And when the flat was empty, old Mr Ehlers climbed into the

 14

van and then, last of all, Carlo the cat got in. Old Mr Ehlers sat with him on his lap. We waved the van off until it vanished round a corner. Grandad suddenly had something in his eye.

It was the first time we'd ever slept alone in the house.

The next morning, we were woken by a hideous crash. The walls shook. The plaster fell from the ceiling. Cracks appeared in the walls. We rushed out of the house in horror. Outside was a digger, crashing a big iron ball into the house walls. The rubble was loaded onto lorries and driven right away.

Dad ran down into the cellar, although Mum begged him not to, and rescued what he could of our lovely nests.

We moved into the shed that was now standing empty in the dusty backyard, and had to watch our beautiful old house being torn down in just a few days.

It was wet and cold in the shed because the November wind howled straight through the cracks.

'We'll have to stick it out here,' said Dad, 'and wait. They're sure to build a new house.'

We'd already seen that happen three times on Paradise Street. They tore down old houses and built new ones, huge concrete blocks with lots of little windows.

We scraped through the winter on the breadcrumbs the builders dropped. We were all bitterly cold and our fur grew scraggly and dull; we could even count our ribs.

CHAPTER FOUR

The new building was finally ready in the spring.

Removal vans drew up and brought the new tenants. We slipped inside while the movers were heaving a heavy wardrobe in through the door.

When we saw the building from the inside, our disappointment knew no bounds: it was all concrete – ceiling, floors, walls and everything. Not a hole anywhere, not even a crack to hide in. All smooth and cold.

And we could no longer get out through the front door because it had an electric exit button which was way out of our reach. So we had to creep around as best

we could under a few forgotten boxes that the movers had abandoned in the cellar.

Not even Mum and Dad had any idea how many families lived in this new building. And the strange thing was that we hardly found any rubbish.

'Where there are people, there's rubbish,' said Grandad. 'That's the mouse's bread and butter.'

There was rubbish. But the people tipped it into a waste-disposal chute and it vanished into a container in the cellar. And we couldn't get into the room with the container.

Soon, we were even hungrier in the new building than we'd been in the draughty wooden shed. At least then we'd had the builders' crumbs.

One evening, Mum reached a decision. She crept very cautiously up the cellar steps and ran down a long corridor. But suddenly one of the flat doors opened, a woman came out and switched on the hallway light.

The woman almost stepped on Mum's tail and froze. Then she screamed: 'Miiiiiiice! Veeeeeermiiin!'

The caretaker came running. Other tenants darted out of their flats.

'Mice?' they cried. 'What? Mice? In this building?'
'Outrageous!'

Then the people, who normally walked past each other in silence, started talking.

The caretaker said, 'I'll get those cheeky interlopers destroyed!' (He really said that – *interlopers*!)

We ran to our cardboard boxes and hid under them as well as we could.

'Now,' said Grandad, 'a cat will come.'

And the way he said 'cat' gave me goosebumps.

Until then, there had only been one dog living in the house, a greyhound, thin as a rake and an elegant bundle of nerves, and also so self-absorbed that he didn't even smell us mice.

But if a cat came into the building . . . the consequences were unthinkable. Like I said, there were no holes anywhere in that place.

Oh, what good times we'd had with old Carlo the cat and Isengrim the poodle.

But no cat came. On the contrary. The next day, the caretaker actually put a lump of bacon in the cellar.

It was all Grandad could do to stop us children from gnawing on the bacon. He explained to us how a mousetrap works. And when we didn't believe him, he poked the bacon with a stick. Snap! A metal clamp slammed down and snapped the twig in two.

At the first opportunity our family fled out of the building.

The backyard had changed too. There was now a boring, neatly-trimmed lawn. The two elderberry bushes had been hacked down and a low hedge planted in their place. The shed had been completely torn down.

In the end, we found a ventilation shaft in one of

the outside walls with a narrow crack that you could climb into. Here we were safe from cats and the caretaker, at least, but good grief, that vent was uncomfortable. It was all clad in sheet metal and there was a constant freezing breeze blowing through it.

But still, we had a roof over our heads.

CHAPTER FIVE

As there was nothing for us to eat in the building, we had to go foraging around the neighbourhood: Mum, Dad, Grandad and us mouse-children.

I often went to the station. It was a long way and not without dangers, because there were a lot of cars on the streets. But you always found lots of good things at the station: binned bread, chips and, now and then, a scrap of cheese. Sometimes, when he felt well enough, Grandad came too. Then we'd run cautiously along the tracks and the platforms where the people stood waiting for trains.

'You see those trains?' said Grandad. 'They travel all around the world.'

'Do they even go to Switzerland? To mouse heaven?'

'Yes, they go to Switzerland too.'

At least you could dream here, at the station. I imagined myself in a factory: a qualified cheese-nibbler, gnawing beautiful holes in the Swiss cheese and keeping them so neat that nobody could even see the tooth marks.

Then, in the evenings, I lay freezing in the air vent. Not even a nest of the thickest fabrics could keep out the cold draught.

Mum kept saying: 'We've got to get out of here, and fast. We have to find somewhere else!'

But where?

The old houses on Paradise Street were already home to well-established mouse families and they guarded their nests jealously.

The new buildings were often even worse than ours. Their cellars were regularly squirted with something they called Insta-kill Spray – if it got you, you'd be a dead mouse.

That was how Isolde lost her parents. One evening, Mum saw a little mouse wandering around the road, crying. She told Mum that the caretaker had just carried her parents out dead. She had no family left. So Mum brought the girl-mouse, whose name was Isolde, home to us.

Once Isolde was living with us, I generally went to the station with her. We'd got to know a snack stall at the station where there were lots of tasty things lying on the floor – chips, for example. Unfortunately, they were often spoilt with ketchup, which the humans are unaccountably fond of smearing on them.

Of course, it was much more fun to stroll around the station with Isolde than with Grandad.

25

We often snuggled down under the platform edge and listened to the announcements on the loudspeakers: 'Please take care on platform fifteen. The train to Paris is about to depart.'

'Paris,' I said. 'That sounds so good.'

And we would watch the train's wheels roll past.

CHAPTER SIX

And then, one Friday, just before Christmas, it happened. Isolde and I had crept onto a platform. It was already dark.

We'd found cake crumbs by a luggage carriage that was already loaded with cases and packets. They'd fallen out of a Christmas parcel that had burst open. A trail of crumbs led from the platform to the carriage.

It wasn't just hunger that drove me into the carriage – I was curious too.

While Isolde gathered up the crumbs outside, I looked around the carriage. There were piles of suitcases and parcels, and a pair of skis by the wall.

A door stood open. You could see through it into the next carriage. I slipped through.

This carriage had lots of compartments and each compartment had six seats. It was lovely and warm. I just wanted to lie down and rest for a moment before going back out into the cold.

When I woke up, everything was jiggling and juddering. I could see lots of legs and shoes. Cautiously, I peeked out from under the seat: humans were sitting there, reading newspapers. Outside the windows, lights whizzed past in the darkness. It slowly dawned on me that I wasn't dreaming, that I really was sitting in the train and that it was moving.

After the initial shock, I told myself that the train was bound to come back to Munich. What I couldn't have known at that time was that all railway carriages have a home station. The carriage I was sitting in came from Hamburg and had only been attached to the Munich train to replace a broken one. Normally, this carriage did the Hamburg-Cologne route. It was just as well I didn't know about that then as I sat chirpily under the seat, eating crumbs that fell from the people's

28

sandwiches. Now and then, the train stopped. I heard the stations being announced: Göttingen, Hanover, Lunenburg, Hamburg.

In Hamburg all the remaining humans got out. I could run at my leisure from one end of the carriage to the other. I found all kinds of tasty things: a chocolate biscuit, a lump of cheese sandwich and loads of bread and cake crumbs. There was enough food for three whole mouse families in that carriage. And there were wonderful hiding places. I made myself a nest in the cladding around a pipe.

I should just add, for the benefit of anyone planning a similar journey, that in wintertime you shouldn't get too close to the heating pipes. It's only too easy to singe your fur.

I padded out my corner with a camel-hair scarf that someone had left behind. I could see a window through a crack in the cladding, and through the window I could see the sky. So I always knew what the weather outside was doing.

CHAPTER SEVEN

Day after day, week after week, I travelled to and fro between Hamburg and Cologne. If there was nobody in the carriage compartment, I climbed up onto a seat and looked out of the window: snow-covered fields; low, squat houses; mountains, rivers, bridges; three milk cans standing at a junction. Everything rolled slowly by.

So this was the wide world. It was so beautiful.

I was only sad occasionally, when I thought about my parents and my brothers and sister, and about Isolde. It would have been so lovely to travel through the world with them, warm and full, and safe from cats.

But I didn't often have much time for sadness because there were always new people getting on. Then suitcases were shoved and heaved onto the luggage shelves and I was staring at legs – women's, men's and children's – and it was raining bread and cake crumbs again.

Soon I knew which city would be next even before the train slowed and a loudspeaker voice announced the station: Hamburg, Hanover, Bielefeld, Dortmund, Cologne and back. So it went on: out one day and back the next. And I kept on hoping that the carriage would eventually be attached to an engine that would take it back to Munich. I could already recognise the ticket inspector by the colour of his trousers and the shape of his shoes. While he clipped the people's tickets, I would sit as quiet as a mouse under a seat.

I spent a good year and a half travelling back and forth on the Hamburg-Cologne line like that – by then I knew every bridge and every barrier.

One day, there were no legs to be seen in the compartment. So I crawled out from under the seats and was about to set to work on a piece of cake that was lying on the floor when, to my horror, I saw a

31

woman. She was sitting there with her legs stretched out onto the seat opposite. She looked at me.

I thought: 'Now she'll scream. Now she'll call the inspector.' But she only laughed and even threw me a few cake crumbs. I made a slight bow and hastily ate the crumbs. Then I withdrew under my seat, keeping an eye on her. She was reading a book and smoking, even though it was the non-smoking section. I'd deliberately chosen a non-smoking compartment because, like all mice, I can't stand cigarette smoke.

In Bielefeld, a man got in and sat down opposite the woman. He struck up a conversation with her and asked where she was travelling to.

'Switzerland,' she said, 'to Basel.'

Switzerland, I thought, how lovely. This woman's heading to mouse heaven. The land of my dreams.

And so I decided I would get out with the woman and follow her onto the train that was heading to Switzerland. It was dark outside, which would surely help with my plan. It was certainly very adventurous to climb off the train, run across a platform and get onto another train again.

 32

But 'nothing ventured, nothing gained', as my grandad always used to say.

I crawled back into my nest and said goodbye to all the things I'd collected over time and couldn't take with me: a glass marble, a little silver earring and a tiny dried rose.

CHAPTER EIGHT

In Hanover, the train stopped.

The woman, whose name was Verena, got out and the man passed her suitcase out to her. I clung onto one of the leather straps on the case, and so I reached the platform unseen and in one piece. There, I cowered in a shadowy corner of a little shelter.

There were humans standing everywhere, waiting for trains. Then the announcement came over the loudspeaker: 'Please stand clear on platform seven. The Intercity train to Basel will be arriving shortly. Keep well back from the edge of the platform!'

The train came in. A sleek, yellow-brown train.

34

The brakes squealed, the train stopped. People got off. I saw the woman get on. I plucked up all my courage and ran across the brightly-lit platform, leaped onto the carriage step and clambered up between the enormous trampling feet. I really could have been killed. But I made it to the top unscathed.

I ran along under the heating pipes. What a difference from my old carriage on the cross-country train!

The floor was covered with soft carpet. The seats were wider and upholstered in colourful, striped velvet. It was only now that I realised how loud all the rattling and clattering had been on my old train for the last eighteen months. This train ran smoothly and very quietly. The windows were wider and the glass had a brownish tint. Outside, the lights flashed past through the night faster than I'd ever seen before. You could hear a voice over the train's intercom: 'Good evening, ladies and gentlemen, this is your driver speaking. We have now reached our top speed of two hundred kilometres per hour. I wish you all a pleasant journey.'

And then a wonderful scent filled the carriage. I cautiously followed the smell to the dining car.

Waiters in red jackets were serving people who sat at little tables. I settled down under a table and nibbled on a roast potato that a man had dropped. Unfortunately, I couldn't enjoy my meal in peace because the man's feet were constantly twitching to and fro as he ate. I had to be constantly on my guard so that he didn't kick me.

After I'd dined, I ran along the aisle of the train looking for Verena. The strange thing about this Intercity train was that almost all the humans on it were men. Most of them sat there wearing suits and ties and it was as though they had all agreed to bring small, leather briefcases along with them. It was all very posh and not nearly as much fun as my old cross-country train where everyone was mixed up together – children, men and women, old and young.

And there were hardly any crumbs on the Intercity train. The people here didn't eat in their seats. And if anyone did unwrap a sandwich, he did it sneakily, almost as if he were ashamed. They went to the restaurant car to eat. There was rubbish galore there. But getting to it was dangerous because the doors between the carriages

opened and shut electronically. You only had to pull the door handles gently and they sprang open, shutting with a hiss a moment later. But of course the door handles were far too high for me so I had to wait next to every door for someone going through it. Then, quick as a flash, I ran after them, before the door slammed shut again. I was in a constant state of fear for my tail.

This train was much more comfortable, no doubt about that, but I'd never have managed to travel undisturbed for as long as I did in my nice, old cross-country train.

CHAPTER NINE

At last the train came to a stop. Outside I heard a loudspeaker voice: 'Basel. This train terminates here. All change, please!'

I cheered. I'd reached mouse heaven. I was in Switzerland!

All the humans got off. I was the very last one to climb down from the train. It was dark outside. I hastily ran across the tracks to the courtyard outside the station, where I met another mouse. It was very shaggy and you could see right away that it often slept outdoors, that it had no home.

The mouse introduced itself. 'Wilhelm.'

'Nibbles,' I said.

Wilhelm was a true Swiss country mouse. He'd come to Basel from his farmyard because more and more cats were making themselves at home there. Here, he'd become a typical station mouse of the sort you meet anywhere in the world. They have plenty to eat so they're well-fed, but because they don't have a proper home, they look pretty shabby.

I asked Wilhelm where the nearest cheese factory was.

'Thass not far,' he said, 'but a mouse would have no chance. None of us gets in no more.'

'Really?' I asked in amazement. 'So who eats all the holes out of the Swiss cheese?'

'Oh,' said Wilhelm, 'thass just a fairy-tale. Per'aps that used to be like that but it's all machines that do that now. There's no room for us moice. Y'know,' he went on, 'Switzerland's no country for moice. It's all too neat and tidy.'

'Watch,' he said. He pointed to a woman standing by a snack stall. She'd just dropped a chip. She immediately bent down, picked it up with her fingertips and carried

40

it to a dustbin. The bin had a catch fastener. You'd never manage to squeeze in there.

'And I thought Switzerland was mouse paradise,' I said.

'Thass a nice old wives' tale,' said Wilhelm, and he told me how mice had to scrape by, getting hungry in this country. He'd have emigrated to France long ago if he hadn't been so scared of travelling by train.

'To France?' I asked.

'Yis,' said Wilhelm. 'Swiss moice in the know are all a-going to France.'

'Well, why don't we go to France then?' I said. And I told him that I'd spent months travelling from Hamburg to Cologne and back in an express train.

'Bootiful!' he cried. 'Let's go!'

CHAPTER TEN

We ran across the platforms until we heard an announcement saying: 'Attention, passengers for Paris. The Trans-Europe Express from Basel to Paris will shortly be departing from platform ten. Please board the train now!'

We ran to platform ten. There stood the train in a solemn shade of blue. We just had time to climb into a carriage before the automatic doors closed.

This train was even smarter than the Intercity. The seats were wide and comfortable. The headrests had white lace antimacassars on them. There was plush carpet in the corridors. I hid under the box for the

heating pipes, but Wilhelm was so amazed that he ran right out into the corridor and was almost trodden on by a human. The startled man was so shocked that he yelled, 'A mouse! Watch out! There's a mouse on the train!'

Someone called for the conductor. People popped out of their compartments. Wilhelm sat in the corridor as if rooted to the spot.

'Come on!' I shouted. 'Quick!' I ran into a compartment and crawled under the seats. Eventually, Wilhelm got away too. We hid right back against the wall.

The conductor came running and the man told him that he'd just seen a mouse, sitting as bold as brass in the gangway.

The conductor didn't know what to do. 'I've never caught a mouse in my life,' he said.

In the end, he called the train driver.

The train driver came. He was wearing a red leather strap across his chest and over one shoulder like a badge of office.

'What?' he said. 'A mouse on the train? Impossible.

Where would it get in from? I've been driving trains for twenty years and I've never seen a mouse on a passenger train.'

He ordered the conductor to look under the seats for the mouse.

We saw two knees, then a huge hand resting on the floor, and then the upside-down face of the conductor, all red and pinched. We looked each other in the eyes.

'Incredible,' he said, and the red face disappeared again. 'There really are two mice sitting under there.'

'Catch them!' ordered the train driver.

'Catch them,' repeated the conductor. 'Certainly,' and his face appeared again.

The big hand reached out for me. I just took a little step to the side and it missed me. He was so clumsy! He tried to grab me again, and again he missed.

'Beasts!' the conductor swore. 'Filthy little beasts!'

He lay down on the floor, all the better to try and catch us.

I whispered in Wilhelm's ear, 'Look out, when he swipes at you, you jump to the left and I'll run straight into his face. Attack is the best form of defence.'

The conductor stayed on the floor. There were lots of feet all around him. The conductor held his breath, concentrated hard and then grabbed for Wilhelm. But Wilhelm was quicker – he jumped aside and I ran straight at the conductor's red, sweating face. Startled, he jerked his head up. There was a resounding crack on the edge of the seat. He yelled 'Ow!' and jumped up. 'A biting mouse!' he screamed. 'That means it's rabid. It's infectious!'

Everyone ran out of the compartment and shut the door from the outside.

Wilhelm and I crawled out from under the seats.

Outside in the corridor there was a throng of humans by the compartment door, peering through the window, all of them men. They stared at us.

'What now?' asked Wilhelm.

'Let them stand and gawp,' I said. 'They've probably never seen mice before. Let's lie down under the seats and have a little snooze.'

We crawled into a corner and stretched out on the fluffy carpet. Wilhelm tossed and turned restlessly but I soon fell asleep.

CHAPTER ELEVEN

A voice on the loudspeaker woke us up: *'Attention, ici Paris, Gare de l'Est.'*

'Quick,' said Wilhelm, 'they're now comin'.'

And so they were – two glowering pest controllers came into our compartment. They got out spray cans and began to fumigate the compartment. So this was the notorious Insta-kill.

'Hurry!' I shouted to Wilhelm. 'Follow me, I know an escape route.'

I crawled into the air-conditioning pipes. I turned back one last time and saw the pest controllers shutting the compartment door from the outside

48

while the blueish clouds of poison filled the air.

We hastily climbed out of the carriage and hid ourselves under the platform.

Once it had got dark, we crept out of the station. Ahead of us lay a wide, brightly-lit street of the sort the French call a *boulevard*.

So this was Paris. The city Isengrim had talked about so much.

'Moice heaven,' murmured Wilhelm rapturously.

We flitted along the house walls. Chairs and tables stood in the open air on the broad pavement outside the cafés and restaurants. Humans were sitting there, in the warm evening breeze, eating and drinking.

That same evening we discovered a particularly glorious French habit. French people like to eat long, straight loaves of bread with every meal. They call them baguettes. As they eat, they break pieces off these sticks of bread. Baguettes could be tailor-made for mice, and so could the custom of tearing the bread because, obviously, they make a lot of crumbs.

49

'If you think about it,' said Wilhelm, 'cuttin' bread don't help us moice much.'

And he was quite right about that.

The French people had another wonderful habit too. There was cheese after every meal, and in so many kinds: long, round and oval cheeses, blue cheeses and white-rinded cheeses and cheeses flavoured with pepper, bay or caraway.

We learned all their names from our friend Pierre, who also categorised them into: *pas mal* (OK), *bon* (good), *très bon* (very good) and *merveilleux* (excellent).

Pierre was a true Parisian mouse. We'd met him outside a restaurant called Les Trois Mousquetaires. Pierre moved along the boulevards without a care in the world. He often said, 'Stride, do not run. People notice scurrying things. But if we walk calmly, humans will not see us.'

So Pierre strolled from restaurant to restaurant, among all the people walking past; he was always on the lookout for delicacies because he only picked up the bread that dropped everywhere as a little side-dish. His favourite foods were truffled *foie gras*, Camembert from the Côte-d'Or and olives preserved in red wine.

There were plenty of olives on the ground because American tourists mostly dropped them under the tables thinking they'd gone off.

'*Les Américains ont une culture de ketchup,*' said Pierre as he nibbled on an olive. That meant 'Americans have a ketchup culture'. Pierre was very strict on matters of taste. 'One can always learn taste,' he'd say, 'otherwise we would still be simple fieldmice, would we not?' And then he'd add, 'And one must have a love for danger.'

CHAPTER TWELVE

Unfortunately, rich as Paris was in pleasures, it held just as many perils. Never in my whole life have I seen so many cats as there were in Paris, and they were the biggest, fastest and fiercest specimens you can imagine. It was in Paris that I first understood the true meaning of the saying 'A cat in the house spells fear for a mouse.'

And the French seemed to be very fond of cats because each house was apparently home to several of them. Yet those cats were kept so short of food that mouse-hunting was always on their minds.

In only our second week in Paris, I had a dreadful thing happen to me.

I was sitting under a table on the pavement, enjoying a piece of brie that someone had dropped during their meal. Suddenly, I felt a shockwave. As I jumped up, out of the corner of my eye I saw a huge black cat hurtling towards me.

I ran for my life.

I could already feel the cat's hot breath on my neck when I spotted a cluster of dustbins on the pavement. At the very last moment, I was able to slip into a narrow gap between two bins. I collapsed, entirely out of breath. The black beast was trying to pull me out with its paw. I crawled further back. What gigantic claws it had! I found myself thinking about good old Tomcat Carlo. But what was this commotion? The dustbins were trembling. The creature was leaping at the bins and trying to knock them over! Fortunately, they were full to the brim with rubbish. The cat was in a frenzy. I think now that it was overcome by the ancient hatred that all predators feel for peace-loving rodents.

Suddenly, to my surprise, the cat just sat calmly down in front of the bins.

53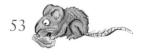

'Fine,' I thought, 'you'll have a long wait there.' And I made myself comfortable.

But then I heard the clattering. A clattering coming from the dustbins that had been put out all over the pavement. And I could hear the rubbish lorry and the refuse collectors carrying the bins to the lorry, emptying them and rolling them back to the houses. The closer the clattering and rolling of the dustbins sounded, the greedier the cat's grin grew. Now it had stood up. Now it was shifting excitedly from paw to paw. Now I could hear the men's voices and the rattle of the lorry. Then the first bin was carried away. The cat was standing right next to my bin, which might be picked up at any moment.

Two men came and lifted the bin. In my despair, I jumped onto one of the men's trousers and ran around his leg like a squirrel. The cat made a gigantic leap after me, clung onto the fabric of the trouser leg and tried to follow me around it. The binman dropped the bin and gave the cat a mighty kick.

'Those fleabags get cheekier every day,' he said, 'they're even attacking people now!'

 54

The cat limped away.

I climbed cautiously down from the binman's trousers and ran home to where Wilhelm and I were living under a phone box. There I sat, with all four of my paws trembling. My heart was pounding and I thought back to how lovely it had been in the old days, in the yard with the elderberry bushes and Carlo, Isengrim and my family.

When Pierre and Wilhelm arrived, they found me all puffed up from crying.

'What's up?' asked Wilhelm.

I told them about my experience with the enormous black cat.

'*Bof*,' said Pierre, 'one must have a love for danger. But look,' he said, 'here, in return, are the advantages of Paris.' He had brought a big piece of camembert with him, which he now gave to me.

'Thanks. But I'd still rather live in Munich. Even if things aren't like they used to be. It's better to be cold but safe in an air vent than to be chased by the monster cats here.'

Even Wilhelm agreed that Switzerland might be no country for *moice*, but he'd rather go back there than stay here in cat-ridden Paris.

CHAPTER THIRTEEN

We bade farewell to Pierre on a Friday evening. Pierre had put together a last opulent meal: *foie gras*, brie and marinated olives.

We sat together until late into the night, eating and drinking, and chatting about a world without cats.

Then we embraced Pierre and ran towards the Gare de l'Est. The last time we saw Pierre, he was strolling with his incomparable nonchalance down the boulevard towards our restaurant Les Trois Mousquetaires.

At the Gare de l'Est, we ran across the tracks in search of a train to Munich. We'd spent long enough at

stations to know that even a mouse should never walk across the tracks. The safest place for mice, though, is right beside the rails, where you're well out of the way, even from the hot water that sometimes gets drained out of the restaurant cars.

So we crept along the rails until, suddenly, we heard mice squeaking. Cautiously, we climbed up onto the platform. The squeaking was coming from a yellow circus caravan standing on a flat goods wagon. A man was just getting out of the caravan. The man had a splendid red moustache.

I said to Wilhelm, 'Wait there, I'll ask those mice where the train's going.'

In the circus caravan, there were several crates and cages, one of which was a large glass case with lots of white mice bustling around inside it. Right by the door there was a little cage with gilded bars. Sitting in it was a dapper white mouse.

'Does this train go to Munich?' I asked.

'Yes,' he said with a sly grin.

Why was he grinning?

Then the train gave a jolt.

'Quick!' I called to Wilhelm. 'Get on!'

Wilhelm climbed aboard, just as the train started to pull away.

'Wass all this then?' asked Wilhelm.

'This is the famous Circus Salambo,' said the white mouse in the golden cage, swaying on a little swing.

'And why aren't you in the glass box with all the other white mice?' I asked.

'Good gracious!' said the white mouse. 'With that common rabble? No, *thank you*. I'm Jack, and I work with the famous conjuror Clandestine. Those mice in the glass case just pull a chariot around the ring, which hardly requires great artistry.'

At that moment, the air shook with a hideous roar.

'Thass a right big cat!' cried Wilhelm in horror.

Jack laughed. 'No, that's Petz, a brown bear. He sleeps most of the time, and sometimes he talks in his dreams.'

'Canada,' we heard the bear mutter, 'Canada.'

'He's dreaming about his forests again,' said Jack.

'Petz is from Canada. And now he rides a scooter round the ring.'

The train stopped and the caravan was pulled off the wagon.

'Is it far to Munich?' I asked Jack.

'I should think so,' he said, grinning again.

Wilhelm and I walked over to the glass case, where the white mice were playing hide and seek. They were squeaking with pleasure.

'They're very jolly,' I said to Wilhelm. 'But I wouldn't like to live in a box like that all the time.'

'No,' said Wilhelm, 'nayther would I.'

CHAPTER FOURTEEN

Suddenly, the caravan started to sway. You can be thrown around in a railway carriage if the driver takes a corner too quickly, but this slow up-and-down movement was completely new. Wilhelm climbed onto a crate and squinted out of a little window.

'Water,' he said. 'Nothing but waa-ter.'

I climbed up and looked out. And indeed, there was green water as far as the eye could see: the sea.

'Where are we a-going?' asked Wilhelm anxiously.

'To England!' cried Jack. 'On a ferry to England!' And he roared with laughter.

Wilhelm and I started to cry. How on earth could

we ever get back across the water?

'You'll have to swim,' laughed Jack, wiping the tears of laughter from his eyes. 'Swim! That's no problem for grey mice like you. No,' he said, starting to laugh again, 'oh, it's too funny. Simply glorious.'

'He be right naughty,' said Wilhelm, 'and a gloater.'

The white mice in the glass case had stopped playing.

'Don't listen to him,' they called. 'Don't let Jack tease you. Come to us!'

We went over to the glass case.

'I'm Tissy,' said a girl-mouse. 'Where do you two come from?'

'I'm a house mouse from Munich,' I answered. 'My name's Stefan but everyone calls me Nibbles.'

'An' I'm a fieldmouse from Switzerland,' said Wilhelm.

'You know what?' said Tissy. 'If you stay with us, eventually the whole circus will go back to Germany. Climb up onto the bear's cage and then jump down into the case with us.'

'What if the bear wakes up?'

'He won't wake up.'

Wilhelm and I clambered up on two of the bars. The case was below us. Yikes, it was a long way down.

'Come on, jump!' cried the white mice, who had all lined up against the glass wall to give us enough space to land in. I jumped first, then Wilhelm. All the walls of the case were made of glass, and they were too high to climb out. It was a big glass prison. But the floor had a warm carpet of sawdust and there was an array of dishes with plenty of food.

'Right comfy,' said Wilhelm, 'but what if we hafter live in this ole box for ever? You can see everything through that glass.'

'Yes,' I said. 'I wouldn't want to live here for ever.'

'How do you stand it in this here glass box?' asked Wilhelm.

'Oh,' said Tissy, 'we were born here and so were our parents and grandparents before us. We're very happy here.'

'And what do you do in the circus?'

'Mr Salambo's famous mouse show. Twenty white mice pulling a cat around the ring on a little chariot.

Look, over there in that basket, that's the cat. Her name's Lena.'

'Ent that dangerous?' asked Wilhelm.

'A bit,' said Tissy, 'but Lena gets such a good meal before every performance that she's pretty sleepy.'

Then everyone thought about how to help us.

'We can hide you easily enough,' said one white mouse, 'in the house.' In the case there was a little house with tiny doors and windows. 'But Mr Salambo comes and picks it up at least every three days, because that's when the whole case is cleaned out.'

'All of us could pile on top of them and hide them under our bodies,' suggested another white mouse.

'Yes,' said Tissy, 'that would work as long as we're travelling. But Mr Salambo will spot them by the time of the first performance, if not before, when he takes us out of the case.'

There was a worried silence as everyone thought.

'Canada,' murmured the dreaming bear. 'Canada.'

'I've got an idea,' said Tissy. 'You know what? You need to learn some little trick so that Mr Salambo will keep you in the circus. The best thing would be if one

of you could learn to run along a tightrope. I have to do that by myself at the moment.'

Tissy climbed up a little pole. There was a thread strung between it and another pole. Tissy said she had to spend several hours a day practising. The other mice used little wooden exercise wheels for their training.

'We need to be very strong,' said the white mice, 'because Lena is a pretty fat cat.'

CHAPTER FIFTEEN

Over the next few days we, Wilhelm and I, tried to crawl along the rope. But it's a pretty unusual thing for house- and fieldmice to do. And so we hung like wet sacks from the tightrope, upon which Tissy could dance so lightly, and which she hung from so gracefully.

On the third day, Wilhelm gave up and said he'd rather practice somersaults because he was used to rolling head-over-heels down the furrows in fields.

I kept grimly on with my tightrope training though.

Every time Mr Salambo's enormous moustache appeared over the case and his hairy hand reached in to pick up the house and change the sawdust, Wilhelm and

I dived into a corner, and all the white mice piled on top of us. That meant that Mr Salambo couldn't see even a scrap of our grey fur. Everything was spotlessly white. Jack almost split his sides laughing, every time.

One day, the caravan stopped. The crates were unloaded. The bear woke up and asked, very sleepily, 'Where are we, eh?'

'In England,' said Jack. 'In Bristol.'

'What miserable weather,' said the bear. 'It keeps raining.'

But he hadn't even opened his eyes – outside, the sun was shining.

The circus people had put up the tent. It was only a small tent, and pretty shabby. There was already work being done in the ring. Mr Salambo's two boys were juggling empty beer bottles. Mr Salambo (whose real name was Gruber) cracked his whip and made the bear scoot round in circles. Every time the bear pushed off with his back paw, he muttered 'Canada, Canada.' Up above, in the big top, Mrs Salambo was swinging on a trapeze.

The only performer who wasn't a member of the

Gruber family was Clandestine the Conjuror. He was already working his black magic on a few bystanders, picking their wallets out of their jacket pockets or pinching the watches off their wrists without them even noticing.

And then came the moment we'd been fearing all that time. Mr Salambo set up a small chariot at the edge of the ring, sat the cat in it and began to pick the white mice, one by one, up out of the case and fasten them into a tiny harness. Wilhelm and I lay on the floor in the corner, feeling one white mouse after another being lifted off until Mr Salambo could see us.

'Huh, what's this?' he said. 'Grey mice. How did they sneak in here?'

His hairy hand grabbed Wilhelm, quickly and confidently.

Wilhelm squeaked anxiously, 'Oi can do roly-polies.'

But Mr Salambo couldn't understand him. He had already reached out for me with his other hand when Tissy whispered in my ear, 'Quick, show him what you can do!'

Hastily, I climbed up onto the rope and ran along

it to the middle, where I wrapped my tail around the thread and let myself fall. I was now swinging in the air by my tail, like Mrs Salambo on the trapeze.

'Wow,' said Mr Salambo.

Then he looked at Wilhelm, still held in his fist, and set him very carefully back in the glass case. Wilhelm immediately did a somersault.

'Wow!' said Mr Salambo again.

He called up to his wife on the trapeze, 'Come and look at these grey mice. We absolutely have to fit them into our routine!'

My goodness, we were overjoyed at that.

Tissy hugged us. And all the other white mice cried, 'Welcome! You're circus stars now!'

CHAPTER SIXTEEN

We made our first appearance in the circus tent on a Saturday evening. It was all very grand. Mr Salambo's daughter rode into the ring. She was wearing a white dress embroidered with glittering crystals.

Then a clown played a little trumpet. He fell over into the sawdust covering the ring. And once he'd stood up again, he blew clouds of sawdust out of the trumpet.

'Dratted trumpet,' he said, and fell over again. He stood up and shook sawdust out of his ears. The audience laughed and clapped.

It was only once the clown was behind the curtain, taking off his make-up, that I recognised Mr Salambo.

Meanwhile, his sons ran around the ring on stilts, each balancing four raw eggs on a spoon in his mouth.

After that, Mrs Salambo did tricks on the trapeze and rode a tiny bicycle across the tightrope. The bear came on with his scooter, still muttering, 'Canada, Canada.'

And then Mr Salambo entered the ring and declared in English with a strong accent, '*Meine Damen und Herren*, ladies and gentlemen, I have ze pleasure to present to you a very famous act. An act that defies ze laws of nature, zat denies ze vork of ze famous Zir Isaac Newton. Incredible but true, vhat you are about to see. A cat pulled around ze ring by twenty mice.'

He set the chariot at the edge of the ring. Then he lifted the mice in their delicate harness from the glass case and fastened them to it. After that, he took the sleepy and very full cat from her basket and set her in the chariot. Lena was wearing a little toga and looked like an ancient Roman. And, last but not least, came Wilhelm – this was Mr Salambo's flash of inspiration – who was placed on the little driving seat directly under the cat's nose. Wilhelm had to hold the little reins in his paws.

 72

'Oi hope that cat has ate enuff,' said Wilhelm as we parted.

Imagine the scene: twenty white mice, driven by a grey mouse and, behind them, the cat in a white toga. Quite magnificent.

Mr Salambo cracked his bear-whip and in a flash, the white mice set the chariot moving. They raced around the edge of the ring so fast that the cat had to cling onto the chariot with her paws. They did three laps like that.

The spectators clapped and Mr Salambo carried the cat back to her basket. The white mice and Wilhelm were returned to the glass case, where they immediately began eating.

Mr Salambo stepped back to the centre of the ring and said, 'Now, ladies and gentlemen, our latest attraction, a vorld sensation, truly. Two fearless mice at extreme height vill show you their tricks and all entirely vithout a net!'

It grew quiet in the tent.

Mr Salambo picked Tissy and me up out of the glass case. Mrs Salambo had sewn a dark blue dress for Tissy and a white suit for me. Tissy and I climbed up a long,

thin bamboo cane. When I reached the top, I looked out at the rows of spectators. The humans were packed tightly together, and hundreds of eyes were looking at us.

Then I stepped on to the thin nylon thread, and Tissy followed. The tightrope was see-through and very fine, and the spotlights were very carefully arranged so that it looked as though Tissy and I were walking on air. In the middle of the tightrope, I wrapped the tip of my tail around the thread and let myself drop. The humans screamed. But then I swung by my tail in the air, as if an invisible hand was holding me.

The difficulty with this routine was that I could only get upright again with a powerful swing. So I had to get myself swinging like a pendulum. Tissy helped by holding out her tail so that I could pull myself back onto the rope. We ran back across it. The audience went wild, cheering enthusiastically. We climbed down the bamboo cane. Mr Salambo put us carefully back in the glass case.

After us came Clandestine the Conjuror. He was dressed all in black and carrying a top hat. He threw

four metal rings up in the air, one after the other, and when he caught them again, they were linked together, yet nobody could find any way of pushing one through another.

Then he brought out his magic jug. Using just the one jug, he could pour each person a drink – whatever they wanted: tea, red wine, carrot juice, coffee, gin, or even a special liqueur that sparkled with flecks of real gold!

Next, he put the jug away and pulled a white rabbit out of his top hat.

For the grand finale, he asked a woman in the audience to pass him her handbag. He asked her if she liked mice.

'No,' she said, 'definitely not.'

'So why have you got a white mouse in your handbag then?'

And he pulled Jack out of the bag by his tail.

The people clapped and shouted, 'Bravo!'

Wilhelm said, 'That Jack and that Clandestine are real artists, you got to give 'em that.'

CHAPTER SEVENTEEN

So, days and weeks passed. We travelled from one English town to another. Autumn, winter and spring came and went, and then it was summer again. We hardly even noticed the cold seasons, it was so warm in our case. There was plenty of food and no fear of cats, apart from during our appearance in the ring each evening.

Wilhelm said, 'I'm right afeared every evenin'. Sooner or later, Lena won't have ate enuff, or she'll get all grumpy, an' then, gulp, that'll be the end o' me.'

As for me, the more times I did my trick on the tightrope, the more scared I got: scared that one day I'd fall. It was a dangerous height.

Sometimes Wilhelm and I sat in the glass case, looking out. Then Tissy would ask, 'Why do you two look so sad?'

'Just you look out there,' said Wilhelm, 'those bootiful trees, the thick bushes, the grass and the wunnerful black soil.'

And I said, 'D'you know what, Tissy? All the holes and tunnels in a house are just the best. And so are the smells that waft through a building when someone's frying potatoes, or when there's cheese in a room.'

Tissy said, 'You're homesick again,' and she tried to get us to laugh with her.

The white mice couldn't understand our sorrows – they had never experienced life outside the glass case.

One day, we heard that the circus was to travel by ship from Britain to Iceland. Iceland is a big island quite close to the North Pole, where there are huge glaciers. It was a chilling shock to us all. Only Petz, the bear, was glad.

'Wonderful, eh,' he said. 'Iceland sounds good. *Ice-land*. Snow and ice. Glorious. Maybe there are big forests there too, eh.'

Now when he scooted around the ring in his evening performances, he was muttering: 'Iceland, Iceland.'

'What do we do now?' asked Wilhelm. 'The circus ent goin' back to Germany, that's gettin' farther away. If we land up on that old island, I don't reckon we'll see our Switzerland again.'

'We've got to escape from this glass box,' I said, 'before we get loaded on to the ship.'

But how?

All the white mice tried to help us figure out how Wilhelm and I could get out of the case. Tissy thought about it too, although she was very sad that we wanted to go. She often cried. And we were sad too. It was a very odd thing: we wanted to go and to stay at the same time.

'We won't ever get out of here. Them glass walls are so smooth an' far too high. We'll end up sittin' in here all our lives long,' said Wilhelm sadly.

But then I had an idea.

Clandestine the Conjuror was in the habit of laying his coat over our cage before his performance. The coat had a secret pocket. Just before he went on, he slipped

the little white rabbit and the arrogant white mouse, Jack, inside it. Then he walked into the ring. Every time he pulled the rabbit out of the hat or Jack out of a lady's handbag, he actually reached into the coat as quick as a flash and pulled out one of his co-stars. He was so speedy and skilful about it that everyone thought the rabbit had really been in the top hat and Jack had really been in the bag all along.

'I'll tell you what,' I said to Wilhelm, 'straight after our performance, let's creep into Clandestine's coat and, once the show's over and the coat's hanging in the wardrobe, we'll sneak away. Then we head to the port and find a ship that'll take us home.'

CHAPTER EIGHTEEN

On a Friday later that summer, the circus gave its last performance in Hull. The next morning, all the cages were to be loaded onto a ship and transported to Iceland.

'I hope Clandestine will put his coat down on our case tonight as usual,' I said.

We said goodbye to the white mice, hugged them, and everyone cried.

Then came Wilhelm's performance. He whizzed three times around the ring with the twenty mice and Lena, the cat. After that, Tissy and I climbed across the tightrope, and Mr Salambo set us back in the glass case.

Clandestine the Conjuror came and did indeed lay

his heavy coat over our case as he slipped the white rabbit and Jack inside. Hastily, Wilhelm and I crawled in after them, just as the coat was picked up again. Clandestine put it on and hurried out into the ring.

We'd barely reached the secret pocket when Jack hurled himself at us, shouting, 'What are you grey vagabonds doing here? Out! Out! Out!' And he started wrestling me.

The little white rabbit sat, terrified, in the far corner of the secret pocket. While Jack and I were fighting, a hand suddenly appeared and *whoosh!* The rabbit vanished.

Then we heard Clandestine the Conjuror ask, 'Do you like mice, madam?'

A woman's voice cried, 'No, no!'

'My cue!' gasped Jack – I'd just got him in a headlock.

And then it happened.

The speedy hand dived into the pocket and Wilhelm disappeared.

Clandestine the Conjuror said, 'So why do you keep a white mouse in your handbag?'

Then there were roars of laughter. The audience

82

were laughing and laughing. Because the great magician Clandestine was not holding a white mouse: he had a grey fieldmouse by the tail.

The hand returned and shoved Wilhelm into the pocket.

'Uh-oh,' said Wilhelm, his fur standing on end. 'That's ruined it, that have.'

The people were still laughing. Clandestine the Conjuror had walked behind the curtain, and he now pulled the coat off, reached into the secret pocket and pulled out Wilhelm and me.

'You filthy little beasts! I will not be made a laughing stock by you!'

And then he threw us to Lena the cat.

'There,' he said to Lena, 'polish them off!'

But Lena had eaten so much that she just burped and murmured a sleepy, 'Pardon me!'

Wilhelm and I ran for it. Past Mr Salambo, who gave a desperate cry of, 'Stop!'

We ran past Petz's cage. He was mumbling, 'Iceland. Sounds so good! Lovely. Almost like Canada.'

We ran out into the night and listened from a safe

distance as Mr Salambo argued with Clandestine the Conjuror. The last glimpse we had of the circus was the colourful string of lights over the Big Top.

'What now?' panted Wilhelm.

Hmm, what to do?

We needed to get to the harbour. We had to try and get a ship that would take us from Britain back to the mainland. So we crept through the night-time streets towards the sound of the ships' horns.

CHAPTER NINETEEN

Down at the port, it smelled of fish. We carried on, being extra careful because where it smells of fish, you often get cats. Lots of cats. We walked along the quay, where the ships were berthed.

'Jus' imagine,' said Wilhelm, 'if we were to get on a ship thass a-going to America or to Africa.'

'What an awful thought!' I said. 'Although I've always wanted to meet a jumping jerboa.'

'We'd better not then,' said Wilhelm hastily.

We spent three days and three nights sitting in a hole in the harbour wall, watching the ships that came in and went out. The ships were unloaded and reloaded.

But we couldn't make up our minds which of the ships to board. How could we know where they were going?

At night, we huddled together in the hole. How warm it had been in the glass case at the circus! Now our stomachs were grumbling because we didn't dare go out. We kept seeing huge cats stroll past: mangy, feral creatures, dragging away colossal fish.

One evening, we heard two men walking right past our hiding place. One said, 'Why, it's proper dirty here.'

And the other said, 'Aye, it is an' all. Wu'll be back in Hamburg the day after themorra, though.'

They were two sailors, walking towards their ship. As I'd spent so long travelling between Hamburg and Cologne, I was able to translate their dialect for Wilhelm: 'They'll be in Hamburg in two days, and they're happy about it.'

We noticed which ship they went on and climbed aboard after them. We crept through a porthole into the hold.

What a surprise! The ship's hold was full to the brim with wheat. What a dinner!

We had just settled down and startled nibbling on a grain or two when suddenly a big rat loomed over us.

'What are youse doing here?' grumbled the rat.

'We want to get to Hamburg and then on to Munich,' I said.

'Beat it, sharpish, this is our ship,' said the rat. 'It's not for youse landlubbers.'

'Landlubbers!' said Wilhelm. 'Thass a load o' old nonsense, we're moice!'

Hastily, we dived into the mountain of wheat and tunnelled our way deep inside it. There we sat as quiet

as mice. For a while, we heard the ship rat digging around in the wheat, cursing and muttering: 'Dirty beggars, blimey, blimmin' 'eck . . .'

Then it disappeared and everything went quiet. We just stayed put, sitting there in the wheat. It was warm and soft, and we were surrounded by food. It was like paradise.

CHAPTER TWENTY

The ship suddenly began to vibrate and pitch. That was the engine. Soon we could hear the waves outside slapping against the hull. The ship swayed gently. We travelled like that for two days and a night. Then the engines stopped and the ship lay quiet.

'How are we goin' to get out of here?' asked Wilhelm.

'Wait and see,' I said.

After a while, we heard something gurgling like a whale.

'My heart alive, that right scared me!' said Wilhelm.

Cautiously, we worked our way out of the wheat and peeked out. Sticking out of the open cargo hatch

was a thick pipe, into which the wheat was vanishing with a slurp, as if it were a giant straw. Just then, we were sucked up by the airstream and dragged into the tube with the grains of wheat – we whooshed up it and then the grain elevator spat us out into a barge on the other side.

I felt quite dizzy after being shaken up like that. When the barge was full, a tug boat towed it through the port and out into a canal.

'This is Hamburg!' I cheered. 'Look, over there: the tower with the round, green dome, that's St Michael's and there, that roof, that's the main station.'

The barge was tied up at the quay. When night fell, we crept ashore and crossed two wide streets to the station.

It was so lovely to be at a station again. We hid beneath the edge of the platform.

In the morning, a train to Munich was announced. It was due to arrive at platform fourteen.

It was an old train, and very dirty. It reminded me of my old cross-country train on which I'd spent over a year travelling to and fro between Cologne and Hamburg. We climbed cautiously onto a carriage.

'I hope this train really does stop in Munich,' I said. 'What if we ended up in Istanbul? That's in Turkey, somewhere.'

We were almost on the point of getting off again when I remembered that Munich station is a terminus. So the train would *have* to stop in Munich.

We crept through the train. Every compartment was full. Eventually, we found one where a Greek family was sitting: a father, a mother and four children. The father and mother had spent three years working in Hamburg as a binman and a cleaner and now they were going

back to Greece. They had filled the whole compartment with crates and cartons, and there was even a basket with two clucking chickens up on the luggage rack.

Once, Wilhelm accidentally showed himself when he was picking up crumbs, but everyone laughed and the children fed us breadcrumbs. The Greek family sang and we whistled along. It was such a merry journey.

The closer we drew to Munich, the harder it was for me to contain my joy. In the end, I climbed up onto a seat and looked out of the window.

It was almost three years since my accidental departure. Fortunately, nothing had changed. The Frauenkirche cathedral was still there with its two towers and its domes that looked like half-balls of Edam. The sky was blue and the leaves were all the colours of autumn.

CHAPTER TWENTY-ONE

But what a disappointment when we reached Paradise Street!

The mice in the air vent at the flats weren't my family but strangers. They said that my family had moved to the countryside six months earlier. Grandad had got rheumatism from the draught in the vent and Lilyfey had been coughing continually. But nobody knew exactly where they'd gone. They had secretly climbed onto a truck belonging to a farmer who drove through the streets every Thursday selling potatoes.

They told me Dad had said, 'Better to set off into

the unknown than live in this cold new building where we've got nothing to bite or chew.'

The strange mice invited us to stay. They shared the little bit of food they had with us.

It was unpleasantly cold in the air vent, even on a warm autumn day. There was a fierce draught and the metal-lined pipe was slippery and uncomfortable.

The people in the house still threw their rubbish down the chute, where it vanished into the container in the cellar, never to be seen again. The mice told us how hard it was to gather enough food in the local area. I asked them why they didn't go to the station during the day any more.

They said that the route was too dangerous now. Since I'd been away, a motorway had been built, and you'd be risking your life if you tried to cross it when it was busy.

I showed Wilhelm the spot where the old shed used to stand. The lawn in the yard was trampled and brown.

We couldn't possibly stay here. Train travel is much more comfortable and more interesting. But on the other hand, I desperately wanted to see my parents and

brothers and sister again, and Grandad and Isolde too, of course.

Wilhelm and I decided to wait until the farmer came and then we could climb aboard his truck. Maybe then we'd be able to track my family down.

Thursday finally came and that morning we heard shouts of 'Potaaaatoooes, eeeeighty ce-ents a kilo!'

The farmer was coming in his truck.

The truck stopped in the street outside the building and women and men queued up with bags and boxes. The farmer weighed out the potatoes on his scales. It wasn't that easy to get up to the truck unseen because most of the humans were just standing silently, staring into space. I thought about Pierre: *stroll, don't run.*

So, although our hearts were pounding, Wilhelm and I walked calmly across the pavement, past the waiting people and over to the truck. Then we climbed up the tyres and ducked under the tarpaulin.

The truck was full of sacks of potatoes. There were potatoes all over the floor. We hid right at the back, behind a sack by the driver's cab.

The truck set off again, but kept on stopping.

We listened as the farmer shouted out again and again: 'Potaaaatoooes, eeeeighty ce-ents a kilo!'

We heard him drag the sacks across the truck, then the sound of potatoes pouring out and the scrape of his scoop with which he heaped the potatoes on the scales. 'Four euros,' the farmer would say.

We watched with horror as people were buying vast quantities of potatoes and taking them away. The longer it went on, the more he stopped, and the more he sold, the nearer the farmer came to the sack behind which we were hiding. Finally, there was just one potato sack left. The farmer stopped again, got out of the truck, grabbed our sack and shook it out. We just about managed to leap behind two large potatoes. Now he wouldn't spot us.

But then the farmer began to gather up the potatoes lying around on the floor and to sell those too. Then he drove on and I thought, If he stops now and sells the last potatoes, he'll reach for our ones too.

But he didn't stop again; he drove out of the city. He drove like a demon, braked, lurching off again. We had to jump this way and that to keep out of the

way of the potatoes rolling around the floor, or we'd have been squashed.

Oh, how gloriously calm and comfortable train travel is! All the bends and bumps and the stink of petrol made me feel dizzy at first, and then ill. Much longer and I'd have been sick. But then the truck stopped. We'd arrived at a farm.

By the time we climbed out of the truck, dusk was falling.

CHAPTER TWENTY-TWO

'What now?' asked Wilhelm.

'We'll have to ask,' I said.

'Watch out, lad, there be a cat round here,' said Wilhelm, sniffing.

But all we could see was a bat, flitting past overhead. I called out to her and asked if she knew of a mouse family that had moved out from the city about six months ago. The bat flew round a corner and waggled her wings, which presumably meant 'No'.

'Uh-oh!' cried Wilhelm. 'Cat!'

The cat had crept quietly up on us and was now only a leap away. We dashed to the closest hole in the

99

ground we could find. But it was so shallow that the cat could easily have scooped us out with its paw. We crouched down and flattened ourselves to the bottom as much as possible.

This cat was obviously not as sophisticated as the Parisian cats because it just sat by the hole and waited.

'Let it wait,' I whispered.

Time passed. Every time I peeped cautiously out of the hole, I saw the cat sitting outside.

'It ent gone,' said Wilhelm, 'is it?'

We waited ages and ages.

We were starting to think we'd have to starve in the hole if there were several cats on the farm, as Wilhelm

thought, and they were taking it in turns to keep watch.

Then suddenly, we heard a wild barking and the cat hissing.

I carefully put my head out of the hole and saw a dog chase the cat up a tree. The dog stood at the bottom, barking up at it. It was a poodle. Didn't I know him? Yes, I did: it was Isengrim!

'Isengrim!' I cried, running over to him. 'Isengrim!'

It was some time before he heard me, he was barking so loudly and so determinedly at the cat, which was sitting up in the tree, spitting down at him.

'Hello,' he said in the end, 'who are you?'

'I'm Nibbles! Don't you remember?'

'Oh,' he said, 'so you're the lost son! Your parents will be overjoyed.'

'Do you know where they are, then?'

'Yes,' said Isengrim, 'of course. They live at our place now.'

'Our place?'

'Yes, Mr Kringel the artist and I live in a little house here in the village. Mr Kringel bought it back

when our house on Paradise Street was being torn down. It's just back there. And there are no cats in the house – thanks to me, you know,' he added proudly.

I turned to my companion. 'This is my friend Wilhelm; he's from Switzerland.'

'Nice to meet you,' said Isengrim. 'Now, come with me.'

CHAPTER TWENTY-THREE

We walked down the village street behind Isengrim. We saw various cats, but they all kept their distance or jumped hastily up onto walls. Finally, we came to a little old house. There were two elderberry bushes in the garden. Isengrim showed us the entrance to the cellar.

'They live down there,' he said.

We climbed down and found the whole family having their supper. Grandad, Mum, Dad, my brothers, my sister and Isolde – they were all there.

Oh, what joy!

Everyone squeaked with delight and we hugged and

they bombarded me with questions: 'Where have you been all this time? Why did you go off on the train like that? Why does Wilhelm talk so funny? Where have you sprung from?'

But Mum said, 'Let them eat in peace now. We've got all the time in the world for talking.'

ZiPPEL: THE LiTTLE KEYHOLE GHOST

Alex Rühle
Illustrated by Axel Scheffler

Paul returns home from school one day to discover a tiny ghost is living in the keyhole of his front door. He names him Zippel, and the little ghost is curious about everything, from food and clothes to how the toilet flushes! But Paul's parents want to change the locks – can Paul find Zippel a new home in time?

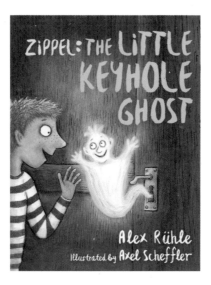